Finding God in Small Places

Faith Sharing Through Changing Stories

By Caroline Ilogienboh

Finding God in Small Places
Faith Sharing Through Changing Stories

Sun Rose Publisher

P. O. Box 2314
East Orange, NJ 07019

ISBN: 978-0-9712781-8-9

Library of Congress Control Number:
2008907567

First Edition

Proof Readers:

Irene D. Foley

Nemedia J. Ilogienboh

All characters in this book are fictional. The stories have no relation to anyone bearing the same name.

Printed in the United States by Morris Publishing
3212 East Highway 30
Kearney, NE 68847
1-800-650-7888

To my bounteous God,

All I have comes from you. I thank you for your generosity. I offer my gifts so that your words may not return void. By the seeds, may yearning hearts find you.

Acknowledgement

I came from a big parish to St. Raphael Church, Livingston, NJ, and fell passionately in love with Jesus.

I thank the wonderful parishioners, especially the daily morning mass group who warmly welcomed me.

"A candle cannot light itself; it needs someone to light it." Thanks to the WINGS, faith-sharing women's group. Your response to the first story I brought to our meeting lighted a candle.

Special thanks to Ms. Ann Peters. Every visit with you is a blessing.

To Nancy Norris and John Zambri, thank you for your support.

To Carmen Baugh, thanks for sharing your thoughts and time to bring this work to fruition.

To Rev. Dr. Eustace U. Edomobi and Rev. Gerald F. Greaves, your homilies are like bulbs that light up the darkness in our hearts. Thank you.

God bless.

Preface

Scriptures tell us that the path to life is through Jesus Christ. Thirsty, we search for him and sometimes miss the mark. The good news is that we can find him. In quiet moments, he speaks to our hearts, and at busy times he speaks to us through circumstances. All we have to do is listen.

"The Gospel contains a *fundamental paradox*: to find life, one must lose it; to be born, one must die; to save oneself, one must take up the cross. This is the essential truth of the Gospel, which always and everywhere is bound to meet with man's protest. ...The Gospel will be a challenge to human weakness. But precisely in this challenge lies all its power. Man, perhaps, subconsciously waits for such a challenge; *indeed, man feels the inner need to transcend himself. Only transcending himself does man become fully human." Pope John Paul II*

Change can be subtle, and sometimes sneaks up on us unanticipated. The stories in this book are of people who in their everyday lives found God in small places or unexpected circumstances. Each of the twelve stories centers around common human functioning which we sometimes take for granted, yet underlies the core of our everyday existence: fear, anger, jealousy, guilt, lust, shame, anxieties, apathy, despair, prejudice, and addiction. The stories present us with thought-provoking examinations of the characters, nudge us towards a reflection on our own lives, and also promote a deeper relationship with God.

FOREWORD

This book is about how our lives in some way relate to many of the trials and tribulations that the characters in the stories face. During our life's journey God is the one sustaining force that will always help us. This should be our focus.

As I read the stories I realized that the situations presented are everyday events. Through the characters we see those unexpected events which will no doubt come our way. When we find ourselves in similar situations we can ask, "How did the characters in the book handle the situation?"

The stories help us reflect on how we have served God. When we retire at the end of the day we can examine our consciences and ask, "Did we satisfy our Christian obligation, or did we fail?" A good example of a helpful story within the confines of this book is when we are called to take a stand on something that is morally wrong, but feel pressured by today's conflicting modern view to take a different position (as in the story of God Can Use You Wherever You Are, page 29.) When our minds wander with inappropriate thoughts is another example (see the story of the Lustful Hearts, page 33.)

Each session has a part one, and after each event there is the question, who are you in the story? Which character most represents you? I learned that I was not always the "good heroine" in the story. This has allowed me to look at my inner-most self and truly reflect on where I have failed God and how I could correct my short comings.

The stories remind us that as Christians it is a struggle to do what is pleasing to God and to reach the point of perfection. We are here to serve God and that is sometimes forgotten. The path to God has been given to us by Jesus. The problem is that we have the tendency to deviate from that path. Jesus offers us redemption. We must always remember that we are here for a reason, and the most important one of all is to have an intimacy with God.

The key to our spiritual journey is prayer and bible reading. Every session in this book ends with bible readings and a prayer. Jesus, by his example, taught us that the way to remain in communion with our heavenly father is through prayer.

The storylines along with certain passages cited from the bible shed more light onto my understanding of the word. I shared the book with various friends. They were enlightened by the examples. We now strive to be a light to those who are in this world and are still in darkness.

Carmen Baugh, Esq.

Suggestions for Small Group Meetings

This book is designed for all audience. A facilitator is recommended. She/he doesn't have to be an expert in bible study, but rather a guide to encourage participation and keep dialogues flowing.

Opening Prayer

A short prayer to open the session will allow everyone to calmly come into the presence of God. Prayer can be said by anyone. Christian music may also be used.

Preparation

Reading the stories before gathering may give individuals opportunity to reflect ahead of time and enhance productive discussions.

Confidentiality

Faith Sharing often involves personal stories. It is of utmost importance to stress confidentiality of information.

Closing Prayer

The sessions end with a closing prayer. This may be time to thank God and also pray for those in need. This will leave individuals feeling fortified with the Holy Spirit as they continue their spiritual journey.

Table Of Contents

A Message for you

In my eyes he gazed.
Gently, he called my name.
"Since when?" I asked.
"Since I first saw you," he answered.
Suddenly, I was raised up and brought to himself.

The weight within me slowly melted away.
Like a flame lifted from a burning log, my spirit floated.
Fiery red it dispatched, illuminating darkness,
Flourishing and abating fear.

This, I bring to you.
It has no measure, no depth, and no limit.
It is simply to say, "You are loved always."

Session 1

Love Your Neighbor as Yourself.

Part 1

In a certain town lived two men and their young sons. There was a blind man, Nelson Bila and his son Henry, and a lame man, Wilson Matt and his son Benny. For months the two men and their sons begged for alms at the local market. The Bila family usually sat at one entrance to the market, while the Matt family took the other entrance.

Wilson began to notice that Nelson collected more money at his location; it was the main entrance and was used by more people. He often went home complaining about the small amount of coins tossed in his plate at the side entrance. Early one morning, he woke up his son and they rushed to the market. He told the boy that they needed to get there before Nelson. He felt it wasn't right that Nelson collected more money than him. On arrival at the market, they were glad to see that the main entrance was unoccupied.

When Nelson and Henry arrived they asked Wilson and his son to move to their usual spot. Wilson refused and they began to argue. The boys decided to let their fathers fight it out by stoning each other. Whoever won the fight got to stay at the main entrance. They each picked up stones and handed them to their fathers.

Nelson was to throw the first stone. He listened briefly to his son, who pointed to the direction at which he should throw the stone, and then threw it. He was completely off course and missed Wilson.

It was Wilson's turn. He threw his stone and it grazed Nelson's ear.

Henry whispered to his father, telling him the exact location where Wilson sat. Nelson made another attempt and this time the stone whizzed past Wilson and landed in the nearby bushes.

People had begun to gather around to watch the fight. They started laughing.

It was Wilson's turn; he balanced on the ground, heaved up his upper body and swung hard, aiming for Nelson's head. The stone struck Nelson's forehead, drawing blood. Nelson doubled over, groaning painfully. He told his son he couldn't continue with the fight.

Agonized by his father's defeat, Henry cried out, "Father in Heaven, to be blind is the worst affliction on Earth." He grabbed his father's arm, holding him tight.

"My son," the father said. "The worst blindness is not of the eyes, but of the heart. Let's get out of here. I have no eyes to win this battle; neither did I know that this location was better than any other when I first sat here."

Perturbed, Henry asked, "You sure, Dad?"

Nelson nudged him to move. "Since the one who has eyes says it is better, let him have it."

Dejected, father and son walked away.

Who are you in this story?

Recall a situation when you were like one of the characters.

Wilson, the lame man (Envious of another's position.)

____

____

Nelson, the blind man (Handicapped in a situation either by physical, financial, intellectual or emotional limitations.)

____

____

The Onlookers (Observed a disorderly situation, yet found it amusing.)

____

____

The sons (Trying to solve a problem but do not have sound decision making abilities.)

____

____

"The worst blindness is not of the eyes, but of the heart."

What is your understanding of this statement?

____

____

How do you react to others' fortune?

____

____

Part 2

The wealthiest man in the town had one daughter. For fear of being kidnapped, she was not allowed to venture out into the town on her own. That afternoon, tired of being restrained within her home, she decided to sneak out of the house. Fully disguised, she set out for the market. Fearful of being discovered, she knew not to use the main entrance. She was walking by the side entrance when the hem of her dress got caught on a nail that was lodged in a protruding piece of wood. Henry saw the incident and immediately sprang into action; he used his father's walking stick to lift the girl's dress, setting it free from the entrapment. The girl was very grateful and rolled out a wad of money. She dropped it into their collection plate. At the end of the day when Henry counted the money, he creamed, announcing to his father that they collected more money than they ever had. The news quickly spread. Wilson heard about Nelson's good fortune and regretted leaving the side entrance.

Nelson was grateful that God was with him even at the side entrance.

Faith sharing:
Where in your life has God surprised you when you thought you'd lost, and he gave you more than you ever imagined?

____

____

Reflections:

Some of us are like the lame man and his son; discontent with what we have, or unhappy when others are successful. Covetousness is a sin (Exodus 20:17). The Matt family thought that the position that the blind man had was the reason for his prosperity, undermining the truth that God choose to favor the blind man. Jesus reminds us in the story of the vineyard workers that the owner can do whatever he likes with his money (Mathew 20:1-15).

God has abundance; he distributes according to his purpose and wisdom. We are to trust that he knows what is good for us.

When we are happy for and with others we pave way for our own success as well. Contentment is not found in money or worldly possessions, but in knowing that God is our source and will not fail us.

Bible Reading:
(Psalm 23:1) The Lord is my Shepherd.
(Obadiah 12- 14) Do not rejoice in your brother's calamity.

(Ephesians 4:22-27) "So get rid of your old self..."
(John 9: 39) Jesus said, "I came to this world to judge so that the blind should see and those who see should become blind."

What kind of cooperative proposal would you recommend to the two men?

____

____

How do we create a new self to live in God's likeness? By:

- Thanking God for whatever position we're in.
- Believing that another person's progress is not the reason for our short-comings.
- Making life in whatever situation we find ourselves. Joseph's brothers sold him into slavery, he went to prison, yet he became a prime-minister in Egypt; Esther became a Queen in a strange land, all because God's will must stand.
- Believing that God has a purpose for our lives.
- Having faith that we will be victorious in our circumstance by acknowledging Jesus as our source and strength.
- Knowing that God will make happen for us whatever we make happen for others.
- Believing that we find joy when we rejoice with others.
- Cognizant that everything we do is a seed that will germinate.

Prayer:

We thank you Father for our lives. We pray to always feel your presence. Give us eyes that see your wondrous gifts on earth.

Session 2

Five Husbands

Part 1

Kim Dumes once won the National Beauty Pageant with her lean and trim figure. That was some twelve years ago. She now glanced at her reflection in the mirror and shrugged. She had yet to reach her desired goal of 115lbs. It had been six months since she set out to lose 49lbs, and she has 20lbs. to go. She hated coming short and berated herself for the last few meals she consumed. Her lack of resistance towards a good cheesecake topped with strawberry and caramel was her undoing. Just the smell of it was enough to make her mouth water. Sad and disgusted with her looks, she grudgingly lifted her gaze from the mirror. She needed to be at the gym, working out. She grabbed her gym bag and headed out the door.

The traffic was free flowing until then she heard a bang, and her car careened to a stop. Though she was shaken, the impact was not life-threatening. The other car had veered away, facing the on-coming traffic. A closer look revealed a woman at the wheel; she sat immobile. There was an infant car seat strapped on the back seat. Kim reached for her cell phone and dialed for help. She wasn't sure what to do but wondered if the woman was okay. She came out of her car and approached the other vehicle. "Are you okay?" she asked the woman. The other woman rolled down her window. She didn't speak but shook her head. Kim noticed that the woman was pregnant. "I called for help," Kim told her. The woman nodded, but didn't attempt to move. Kim looked at the back seat where a baby sat sleeping.

A police car arrived and two officers emerged. Kim was questioned, and then asked to sit in her car. She watched one officer speak into the radio. Why was the woman still in the car? Kim wanted to know. She ignored the officer's instruction to stay in her car and came out. "Is she okay?" she asked.

"We don't know, ma'am," one officer responded. "The ambulance should be here shortly."

Kim's eyes met the woman's briefly before she went back to her car. The ambulance arrived; the woman and the baby were taken to the hospital. Kim gave her driving information to the officers. She was told to pick up a police report in a few days.

She remembered her thoughts just before the accident. She had looked at the large billboard adjacent to the road and had been asking herself why she couldn't look like the skinny model on display.

Who are you in this story?

Kim (Obsessed with physical appearance.)

____

____

The woman in the other car (Trapped in a situation beyond her control.)

____

____

The baby (Calm and asleep in the face of the unexpected.)

____

____

Part 2

Kim saw the woman a few days later at the police station. They were both there to pick up the police report on their accident.

"Hi," Kim said to the woman, and then introduced herself. "Are you okay?" Kim hesitated before telling her their cars had collided.

"Hi," the woman's face lit up on recognizing Kim. "I'm fine. Thanks for asking," the woman responded. "I'm Marian Hills."

"How about your baby?"

"She's fine also," Marian responded, her hand touching her stomach to indicate that the unborn was fine.

"And the one in the back seat?"

"She's fine too."

Seeing no reason to continue the conversation, Kim bade her farewell and walked away. Something else troubled her about this woman. Just before Marian entered her car, Kim ran after her, halting her to stop. It was her eyes, Kim figured out. There was an unusual calmness in them. The same calmness she had seen at the accident scene when their eyes met briefly.

"Yes?" Marian asked lightly.

"I don't know how to say this," Kim stuttered. She was a little embarrassed for bothering the woman. "I noticed you seem unperturbed, even when we had the accident." Observing the woman's keen look, Kim quickly added. "I thought you'd be worried, with you being pregnant and the baby." She caught herself. "I mean babies."

Marian smiled. "I knew Jesus was waiting for us. My husband has just been killed in the Iraq war." She exhaled slowly and added, "We were married four years, and didn't want to have a baby right away. I was afraid I'd lose my figure." She bent her head shyly. "Then when he got called to Iraq. I threw out the pills and luckily, I got pregnant right away. He died not knowing we are expecting a baby." She paused. "Jesus loves me too much to take this gift from me."

"How about the baby in the back seat?"

"That was my sister's. I was returning her home."

"Thank you for telling me," Kim responded graciously.

Kim was thoughtful after they parted. She had almost robbed the woman of her gift, she rebuked herself. The woman had said, 'Jesus was waiting for us.' She wondered if she, Kim, was included in that "us." The answer came to her two days later.

"Thank God, nothing happened to Marian's pregnancy," Kim said gaily after narrating the car accident to a friend. "I'd never have forgiven myself. The guilt would have killed me." A second after she spoke, she paused as a thought penetrated; a quiet voice told her she was included in that 'us.' Jesus saved her from living a life filled with guilt. She was thrilled to know that Jesus loved her enough to intervene at a time when she was busy desiring another's image. A new awakening overcame her; she'd have to stop obsessing over her weight and end comparing herself to every thin person she saw on her way.

Our hearts are where we put importance in our lives. Often times we become slaves to our desires, neglecting other things. (John 4: 4-20) Jesus met a woman at the well. He asked her to go call her husband. When she said she didn't have one. Jesus told her she had had five husbands. Her earthly desires turned into a yearning to know Jesus when she recognized him as the Messiah. St. Augustine said the five husbands could be metaphors for our five senses: Sight, Touch, Taste, Smell, and Sound.

In the story of Kim, can you identify her husbands?

____

____

How has her desire for these husbands affected her life?

____

____

Can you identify Marian's husband/s (Exclude the spouse that died in Iraq.)

____

____

Did she put her needs before God's plan? Explain.

____

____

How can our action affect an unborn child?

____

____

Faith sharing:
What husband/s are you attached to?

____

____

How can you detach from this/these husband/s? Do you want to?

____

____

<u>Reflections:</u>

We sometimes doubt our self-worth and the love of God. His love can be described like this; a child digs a hole in the sand by the ocean. He wanted to empty the water into the hole. After several trips back and forth, he noticed that no matter how much water he withdrew from the ocean, he didn't make a dent in the body of water. He finally gave up saying, "This is too much for me to understand. The ocean will never dry up!" God's love is like that. It is so enormous that it never dries up.

As beloved children of God, we should see ourselves

as God sees us. We should align our desires with his desires for us. He created us in his image.

When we put our hearts in seeking his kingdom we become Godlike; filled with love and goodness. We begin to marvel at his creation and his awesome provision for our daily needs. We see his work around us and are inspired to work alongside with him on earth.

Do you have doubts about your worth? Jesus says fear not, he would break all boundaries to reach you as he did when he encountered the Samaritan woman (John 4: 4-20). He was waiting for her at the well when she arrived. By speaking to her, he broke the rule that Jews didn't speak with Samaritans, and then he spoke to a single woman alone; these were not accepted back then. Nothing held Jesus back from reaching out to her. She was thirsty for water, and Jesus was longing for her soul. He promised her living water, the kind that she'd never thirst again after drinking it. Salvation occurred when she embraced him as the Lord. She then testified to others and brought many people to him. Jesus is waiting for you.

<u>Bible Reading:</u>
(Psalm 36: 7-9) - God's constant love
(Psalm 139:1-18) - God knows our hearts.
(Micah 7: 18-20) Show of God's merciful love.
(John 6:35) Jesus wants us to throw away what is preoccupying our minds and come to him to be filled with living water.

Prayer:

Lord, help us to always remember that you created us in your own image, and all that you are is good. Forgive us for the times when our desires have not been in line with your will for us.

Session 3

Agents of Hope

Part 1

With his head bent down and hands cuffed together behind his back, Dylan Miles walked to a waiting van. It would take him to his new home; a place called "correctional institution."

He went in knowing only what he had been told. That he did something bad and needed to be separated from his family, friends and environment. He had no comprehension of what he did; his sense of right or wrong had never been nurtured to give him a good perception of societal norms.

Growing up, his mother worked a twelve-hour-a-day shift and was too tired to hassle with him when she came home. His father spent most of his time in the gaming room, drowning in bottles; he didn't have the right temperament to wrestle with his rambunctious son. Dylan had learned one lesson from his father, to punch when faced with an uncomfortable situation. That was what had happened when he was confronted at a barber shop.

A fellow customer had jumped ahead of Dylan to take the barber's chair. Dylan seized the fellow's hand, pulling him back. The fellow resisted, and Dylan's fist landed on the man's face, drawing blood and breaking his nose. The barber called the police. Dylan was arrested and charged with aggravated assault which got him a jail sentence.

He went to jail confused and came out more confused because the anomaly in his thinking had been reinforced by the cruelty of fellow inmates. The confused young adult became a lost man and returned home damned.

His mother had no love for him; he was a reminder of her own failures. She tossed him into the streets. His father did nothing but call him a "scumbag."

Dylan roamed the streets looking for direction, but only met desolation and the bitterness of those before him who have now accepted defeat. He joined them to live a purposeless life. One day, beaten and dejected he crashed on the ground, cried out in pain and prayed for death to come, as he had no reason to live.

Who are you in this story?

The mother (Out of a busy schedule she neglected to nurture her child. Or when we are too busy to extend a greeting or helping hand to people around us.)

____

____

The father (Failed in his responsibility to lead his family. He was more married to his game and bottle than to his wife. Or when we're more involved in our own egotistic pleasures than paying attention to others' needs.)

____

____

Dylan (Undernourished in body and spirit. Lost, broken and isolated.)

____

____

Part 2

On Dylan's path came a wounded cat. It sidled by whimpering a low *meow, meow*. Its foot was stuck inside a small can. Dylan looked closely and concluded that the cat must have stepped into the can by accident. It looked to be in more pain than him. He reached for it, and carefully set it free. 'Oh, thank you.' He heard a voice say. Dylan looked up and saw a gentleman standing above him, panting. He looked like he had been running. "Is this yours?" Dylan asked.

"Yes, I've been looking for her."

Dylan gingerly lifted the cat, and handed her to the man.

"Thanks, again," the guy said. He walked off and then returned. Looking around, he uttered, "What's a kind and generous man like you doing roaming around the streets?" He didn't wait for an answer and offered, "Can I buy you some coffee?"

Dylan was thoughtful; no one had called him kind and generous before. The words were warm and soothing. He felt something shift inside him. He stood up, thanking the man for his words and accepted the offer.

Faith sharing:

Have you ever been betrayed by people you love? Or do you know people who pounce on your slightest mistakes?

____

____

<u>Reflections:</u>

We are sometimes like Dylan; dejected and lost. Jesus feels our pain. He was sinless, yet suffered in the hands of people around him. His suffering was even more intense because he foresaw it. His friends abandoned him; people insulted and crucified him (Matthew 27: 27-31). He knows the sting of betrayal and suffering. He walks with us in our suffering.

In spite of any betrayal we are experiencing, the good news is there's hope. St. Augustine said, "What had been lost through infidelity was restored through hospitality." Read the Walk to Emmaus story (Luke 24: 13-32). The men had lost hope because of Jesus' crucifixion. After resurrection they didn't recognize Jesus as he walked and talked with them. Their eyes opened when they invited Jesus to stay with them and Jesus broke the bread.

We learn from Jesus that overcoming all difficulties lies in trusting the reward of God. Jesus suffered mercilessly, yet he accepted death with a meek and humble heart because he knew that the salvation of mankind rested upon him and that God will raise him to glory. We are asked to do the same; in our suffering we should still believe that God loves us.

In the story of Dylan, he found his self-worth when he lost himself. He was able to help the cat when he took his eyes away from his own misery and focused on the cat's pain. For one brief moment when Dylan focused on the cat, he let God enter him to speak to his heart and that brought out the goodness in him. By setting the cat free from its entrapment, he gave hope to it. He in turn received his blessings. We should decrease and let God increase in us; reaching out to others even when all odds seem against us. God desires mercy from us.

Are you too focused on your difficulties so much that you fail to let God in? No matter where you are or whatever discouraging circumstances you face, God has chosen you first. Jesus is waiting for you at the edge. All you have to do is decrease so he can come in. You can be agent of hope.

Bible Readings:

(John 10: 10) Jesus said, "… I have come in order that you may have life in all its fullness."

(John 20: 4-6) At the water's edge the fishermen followed

Jesus' instructions and they caught so many fishes that they could not pull their net out.

(1 Thessalonians 5: 16-17) Be joyous and give thanks in all circumstances.

Prayer:

Lord, we are sometimes so overwhelmed with our problems that we fail to see your presence around us. Do not hold our ignorance against us, but give us the grace to decrease so you may increase in us.

Session 4

Salvation for Death

Part 1

On getting to his home, 15-year old Michael Burns cranked the back door open. With his eyes widened and searching, he scanned the living room, kitchen and den. Everywhere appeared quiet; they must all be asleep, he concluded. He quietly removed his shoes, and closed the door behind him. He entered slowly, careful not to step on anything, lest he'd wake up the household. He tiptoed past his parents' room, and then his grandmother's. He entered his room and breathed a sigh of relief when no one woke up. He knew he'd get into trouble for coming home two hours past his ten o'clock curfew. He quickly undressed and then jumped into his bed.

Grandmother Ethel slept very light; she heard Michael's footsteps. She silently grumbled, cursing the boy and his mischievous ways.

The next day at dinner time, grandmother Ethel watched Michael with uncanny eyes when the boy entered the room.

Full of spirit, Michael greeted, "Hi, Grandma. How're you doing today?"

In her mind, she figured the boy must be happy because he thought he fooled everyone. She responded to him glumly, "Fine." She didn't like his outfit; his shirt had some indiscernible script written on it; his jeans were below the waist with holes on the knees; his hair was unruly. He looked disgusting. 'Don't they teach grooming to kids these days?' she questioned silently.

Michael noticed the gruff expression on his grandmother's face, but dismissed it. He poured himself a full glass of orange juice, even spilling some.

The grandmother whispered something to Laura, Michael's mother. Laura jumped up. "You imbecile oaf!" she yelled at Michael for his disobedience. "You're grounded for life!"

On hearing his son's escapade Nelson, Michael's father, became so infuriated so much that he threw the glass he held in his hand across the table.

On reflex, Michael shifted sideways to avoid the object. While falling backwards and onto the floor, his head hit a wall unit that contained fine china. The glass door shattered and flung open; dinner plates and glasses came tumbling down on Michael. He had several cuts on his body; head, arm and a deep gash on his neck.

The family was immediately upon him, giving him first aid treatment. His mother remembered that he hadn't taken a tetanus shot in over ten years. They decided to rush him to the hospital for further treatment.

Who are you in this story?

Grandmother Ethel

____

____

The mother

____

____

The father

____

____

Michael

Part 2

At the Hospital, Laura and Nelson waited with Michael in the emergency room waiting area. A mother sat in a corner, weeping silently. Moved by the sight, Laura shifted to sit by the woman. She offered some kind words of comfort. The woman thanked Laura, and then spoke about her plight. The ambulance had transported her 13-year-old son to the hospital because he inhaled some household solvent in an attempt to commit suicide. She had found him lying still on the bathroom floor. Torrents of tears ran down the woman's face as she recounted the incident. She blamed herself for not having kept a close eye on her son.

Laura tried to comfort the woman, stating that she should not beat up on herself and to trust God. The agony in the woman's eyes was so deep that Laura felt it tug at her heart. She wondered what had troubled the boy so much that it had pushed him to such tragic measures. Her eyes caught her son's briefly and she wanted to run to him and hold him tight.

After Michael's treatment, Laura glanced at the woman. She was still crouched in the corner, crying. Laura knew she couldn't do much but to pray for her and her son. She exited with one thought in mind: God will take control of the situation. It was as if an inner voice spoke to her too. They had not dealt with Michael's night-out with God's wisdom.

At the Burns' family gathering the next day, the adults sat morosely, each feeling guilty for their part in Michael's injuries. Each of them examined their conscience and viewed their response as a sin.

Grandma Ethel felt she committed a sin in thought by being judgmental, resentful, grumbling silently, and gossiping.

Laura felt she committed a sin in her choice of words and harshness.

Nelson felt he committed a sin in actions by his violent outburst.

Faith sharing:
Are there things you have done where the guilt weighs you down? Are they causing some doubts in your spiritual life?

____

____

<u>Reflections:</u>

Sin puts a distance between us and God and gives the evil one an opportunity to roam in our lives. God desires an intimacy with us, not distance. In our sinfulness we pursue human desires and lose the vision of God's plan for us, which can lead to spiritual death (Romans 8: 5-13).

Jesus says bring all your sins and guilt to him. He who can raise the dead can cleanse any sin; small or big. He raised Lazarus to life (John 11:1-44). He can heal all. He does not hold our sins against us, but invites us to himself. He called Levi, the tax collector, (Luke 5: 27-32). He hung on the cross with his arms stretched so we can have direct access to him. He came so we can be redeemed and put right with God. He has conquered death; sin can not hold us back from the Father's love.

<u>Bible Readings:</u>

(Luke 6: 37-38) On judging others.

(Ephesians 4:26-32) Warning against anger and hurtful words.

(Mark 7: 14-23) It is not the outward appearance that makes a person unclean, but what comes from the heart.
(Ephesians 6: 1-4) Instructions for children and parents.
(Luke 5: 31) "People who are well do not need a doctor, but only those who are sick." Jesus invites us to come to him with our illnesses and be made well.
(Romans 6: 1-11) In Jesus we are alive and dead to sin.
(Isaiah 55: 1-3) God invites us to come to him, listen and live.
(2 Timothy 1: 7-10) Live zestfully with the spirit of God. He will give you a spirit that is filled with power, love, and self control.
(Psalm 98, 100, 117) We do not gain salvation by what we do or do not do. God in his mercy has already given it to us. By his grace we have been saved. Lift up your voices and praise him.

Prayer:
Lord, forgive us when we become judgmental; when our anger, bitterness and actions push us away from you. Share with us the lens with which you look at the world.

Session 5

Faith by Vision of the Heart

Part 1

One morning two teenagers, Katie Mallory and Robert Vobert walked down an alley on their way to school.

"We need to hurry," Robert said to Katie. He didn't like the fact that she seemed fascinated by every little event that happened on their way; she was at it again. He grabbed her arm, pulling her along.

Unaffected by Robert's urgency to move, she shrugged him off. She even came to a complete halt which infuriated him. He grunted and then began to walk away, leaving her to the object of her attraction.

"Don't leave me alone," she mumbled, yet showed no intention of stepping up.

He stopped for a few seconds and then realized she wasn't moving. "Remember what happened to you the last time you were late?" He scowled at her. "The teacher made you cry."

"Look," Katie pointed to a stuffed pillow that lay by a dumpster. Next to it was a dog, pulling on the pillow.

Robert ignored her, insisting that she move. "You're such a stubborn fool. This time you'll end up in big trouble, and I'm not going to cover for you." He left her standing and walked on.

With a keen gaze, Katie leaned forward for a closer look. She let out a loud howl and then began to jump up and down, simultaneously pointing to the loose end of the pillow.

The dog waggled its tail and scooted off.

Robert ran back and bent slightly to see what got her so excited. "Oh, gosh!" he screeched. He needed to do something, but Katie's piercing scream was so deafening that he couldn't think. He threw one hand around her neck and with his other hand placed his palm over her mouth. "Be quiet!" he bellowed, shaking her. When she seemed to get hold of herself, he removed his hands and knelt by the pillow. He slowly pulled back the loose end to reveal what was stuffed inside. It was an infant. He replaced the cover, stood up and looked around. He wasn't sure what he was looking for.

"Do something!" Katie yelled at him.

"I'm thinking," he responded roughly.

The street was sparsely inhabited. On impulse Robert grabbed the pillow, and sprinted on his feet, gunning for the nearest house. Katie ran after him.

Mr. Jim Gunter rocked in his oak chair. Nothing seemed to soothe his aching heart since his wife had died six months earlier. He couldn't eat nor sleep alone; he didn't do any of those things in the fifty years he was married. The loneliness of widowhood was still fresh and he didn't know how to live anymore. He heard the knock on his door, but he ignored it, thinking whoever was there would go away. He wasn't in the mood to talk to anyone. The knock persisted; annoyed, he got up and yanked the door open. He was even more annoyed when he saw two teenagers. They were probably there to sell him something, he concluded. "Get lost!" he yelled at them through the screen door and then closed it in their faces.

The teens were stunned for a few moments. Robert shuttled onto his feet, running to the next house. They didn't wait to be questioned when the door opened. They showed the occupant what they had found, speaking with as much speed as they could muster. They were let in, and the emergency service was called. Assured that the baby would be taken care of, the teenagers left for school.

Pressure from others sometimes influences us to abandon our gut feelings about something. And sometimes it is we who find it hard to trust others' instincts, condemning their actions based on our own prejudices, pain or fear.

Who are you in this story?

Katie

____

____

Robert

____

____

Mr. Gunter

____

____

***Part* 2**

Seven years later when Katie and Robert returned home from college. They assembled together with other residents of the town to watch the 4th of July fireworks display.

"It's nice to see you Katie," Robert said excitedly.

"Hey!" Katie cheered. "Haven't seen you since graduation."

"Didn't come home often. Still picking up strange things?" Robert laughed.

Katie knew he was referring to the baby they had found. She was lost in thoughts for a second and then chuckled before saying, "You almost left. You kept babbling about the punishment I'd get." She gave him a sly look.

"I didn't want to be bothered with a dog minding its business," he threw in.

"Something kept pulling me towards it," she said.

"But when I saw what was in the pillow, I thanked God that you were such a stubborn fool."

"At first it was the hair, and then the head," Katie added. "I remember screaming my lungs out."

"And you wouldn't stop."

"I must have been in shock. A baby stuffed in a pillowcase wasn't something you expected to see on your way to school. Not in a quiet town like ours."

"It was a good thing I was there."

"And you took charge. You were a hero," she said.

"Not really, you were. You saw the dog and the pillow. Even if I had seen it first, I wouldn't have looked at it twice." He added firmly, "You trusted your instinct, even defied the impending punishment I was predicting."

"Thank you," Katie said. "After all these years I finally get a chance to acknowledge your help."

"Do you know what happened to the baby?"

Before Katie could answer the question a group of youngsters came up. It was customary for the town to showcase young talents who entertained the audience before the fireworks began. A youngster took the microphone and sang the national anthem. Everyone applauded him when he was done.

Among the crowd was Mr. Gunter. Watching the fireworks was one of his favorite things. Though still depressed his friend talked himself into coming to the event. Listening to the young man on stage was a delight. The boy reminded him of his son when he was that age.

In fact his son sang that very song many years ago. His mind went back in time, and for the first time since his wife died, his heart bubbled gaily and he smiled. He felt good, and attributed the shift to the young man who sang so melodiously. The boy reminded him that there were still things in life to be happy about. "Bravo! Bravo!' he uttered with vigor as he joined the others to applaud.

Standing beside Mr. Gunter was Robert. "Hi, sir," Robert greeted him.

"He's good, isn't he?" Mr. Gunter turned to Robert.

"You don't recognize us?" Katie asked.

Mr. Gunter looked closely at them, and then shook his head when no recollection came to him.

"Seven years ago, you slammed your door in our faces," Robert said.

Mr. Gunter vaguely remembered. "I don't remember," he quickly admitted.

"We came to your house for help," Robert said.

"We found a baby by the dumpster near your house, and we needed your help," Katie continued.

"We had to run to another house when you told us to get lost," Robert added.

Recollection slowly came to Mr. Gunter; he was immediately concerned, "I didn't know. Did the baby make it?"

Katie who was ever so inquisitive had found out that the baby was birthed by a teenage girl in the high school. The girl's parents had been located and the baby returned to the family. To answer Mr. Gunter's question she said, "He sure did, sir. You were just applauding him."

Mr. Gunter turned to the stage, looking at the boy astonishingly. He had been so wrapped up in his loss that he had almost robbed the boy of his life. And now the same boy gave him laughter again.

On his way home he pondered about the twist of fate. He remembered the scripture verse where Jesus said 'he who welcomes the least of your brothers welcomes me.' He failed to welcome the child when he had an opportunity which meant he failed Jesus; the thought saddened him.

Dejectedly, he told the story to a friend one day. "I feel really bad," he confessed.

"It's a good thing you listened to me and finally went to the fireworks," his friend said. "Had you gone earlier perhaps you'd not have spent so many years in misery."

"Don't you get it?," Mr. Gunter groaned. "I let the boy down, I'm a miserable person."

"No one is condemning you," his friend replied. "So, Jesus came knocking at your door and you blew it. To me it looks like he didn't give up on you, which is why he sent the boy again. If he condemned you, the same boy would not entertain you years later and bring life into you."

Awakening came to Mr. Gunter. "That boy was meant to bring me out of my grief. Jesus must love me enough to try again." He felt a weight lift off his shoulder; he breathed out, thanking God for not giving up on him.

Faith sharing:
Have you been in a situation where you ignored your gut feeling and later regret it? How about when you've followed your instincts?

____

____

<u>Reflections:</u>
God desires our hearts and would try again and again to reach us. Thomas was not with the disciples when

Jesus appeared to them after his resurrection (John 20: 24-28). When Thomas was told that Jesus had risen, he didn't believe. Jesus came back a week later and invited Thomas to touch him and stop doubting. Jesus loved Thomas enough to come back. Just as he did with Thomas, he would come back to us again and again to put our fears, doubts, and restlessness to rest.

Jesus also said, "Blessed are those who have not seen him and believe"(John 20:29). He is telling us to have faith in him. It is by faith that the Holy Spirit comes alive in us. He gave us the Holy Spirit to instruct us, and he asks us to believe when the spirit speaks to us. We are not alone, but joined to God and our brothers and sisters in faith.

<u>Bible Readings:</u>
(John 11: 7-811, 38-43)
Jesus received the news of Lazarus' death; the disciples didn't think it was good for Jesus to go to him. Despite their skepticism, Jesus went to the tomb. Even there, there was an attempt to stop him from doing what he needed to do. He went ahead and raised Lazarus.
(John 8: 11) Jesus loves the sinner, not the sin. When no one threw a stone at the adulterous woman he told her, "I do not condemn you."
(Psalm 46: 1-2) - God's constant presence.
The book of Jonah shows a God who will forgive and save us when we turn away from sin rather than punish and destroy us.

Prayer:
Thank you, God, for your still, quiet voice that resides in us. Help us to know wrong from right. We pray for the Holy Spirit to give us the gifts of wisdom, good counsel, fortitude, knowledge, piety, understanding and reverence. Be with us each step of the way till we meet in eternity.

Session 6

God Can Use You Wherever You Are.

Part 1

One summer afternoon a minister stood at a bus stop, waiting. Along came three adolescent boys, wearing dark colored tee-shirts. Boldly written on each shirt were derogatory remarks about women. The minister read the prints; they were too mortifying and he looked down.

Shortly after, a woman walked in. She saw the boys' shirts and her insides welled with disgust. She glanced at the minister briefly and then proceeded to address the boys. "Young men," she said sternly. "I'm sure you have mothers, sisters and maybe girlfriends." Balancing her hand on her hip and squaring her shoulders, she continued with tightness in her voice. "If you have any respect for the women in your lives, you'd know that what you're wearing is very offensive."

One of the boys geared up to answer her, but was restrained by another.

She stomped her foot on the ground, daring them to come on. She then lashed out in commanding tone, "I suggest you go back home right now and wear something decent."

Observing the woman's tough, aggressive stance, the boys decided against confronting her and left.

On getting to the church, the minister fell on his knees begrudging himself for not having the courage to confront the boys. He felt he had failed in his responsibility.

Who are you in this story?

The minister (Lacking the courage to take appropriate action or had the right idea, but couldn't express it.)

____

____

The woman (Spirited, does not hesitate to speak up.)

____

____

One of the boys (Fulfilling the need to belong or doing the in-thing without being mindful of the impact on others.)

____

____

Part 2

Days later the minister spoke with another minister friend, relaying the incidence and his guilt.

The friend responded with this, "You gave exactly what was required of you."

The minister was puzzled. "That's my point. I didn't do anything," he emphasized.

"You weren't supposed to," the friend calmly replied. To soothe the lingering puzzle on the minister's face, he added. "By your presence, the Lord needed you to be there at that moment to give support to the woman. He sent the one who had the right skill or language to address those boys." He paused.

"Keep talking," the minister prodded his friend.

"Had you addressed the boys, you might have been ineffective in your delivery. Being a woman herself, the new comer took the derogatory remarks more personally than any man could have. She was able to back her words with the right inflections, weight and actions so much that the boys were able to view their behaviors subjectively."

"You mean the boys were able to observe the resultant impact of their remarks on a woman."

"Yes. They also internalized it; through a first hand observation they absorbed the possible effect on their own mothers, sisters or girlfriends."

"Huh," the minister murmured.

"Only through subjective experiences can behaviors be modified; she was able to bring the implications of the derogatory remarks to their consciousness and they felt it."

Understanding came to the minister, and he surmised that when apathy changes into empathy we can affect an individual's attitude towards positive change. He stated, "The woman was able to move them to feel some caring." The friend nodded his head, agreeing with him. The minister felt his guilt lift. "Thank you, my friend," he said and hurriedly returned to the church. He knelt before the crucifix and said, "Thank you, Lord for using me even in the smallest way."

Faith sharing:
In what way have you not seen your worth in a situation?

____

____

Recall what it was like to find peace in your actions or inaction?

____

____

<u>Reflections:</u>

We sometimes fail to see the big picture. God in his infinite wisdom knows our strengths and weaknesses, and he knows when and where he can use us for his purpose. We are God's children; he created us. He put every part of our being together in our mothers' wombs. He knows our thoughts and actions even before we conceive them. He put people in our paths to help us accomplish whatever task he has placed in front of us. All we have to do is trust in him and let him guide us.

He can use us in any situation in big and small ways. An Ethiopian eunuch was reading the scriptures and he didn't understand them (Acts 8:26-40). The Holy Spirit spoke to Phillip, and he approached the Ethiopian caravan. The meeting between Phillip and the eunuch got the eunuch converted and baptized.

All of us are parts of one body in Jesus Christ. When we walk with Jesus we begin to learn how to discern the voice of the Holy Spirit and act according to the will of God.

Bible Reading:
(Isaiah 49: 1-6) The Lord called me from birth.
(Psalm 139) God knows us and cares.
(Mathew 10: 19-20) Jesus gives us the same promise he gave the disciples; not to worry about what we're going to say or how when the time comes.
(Philippians 4:6-7) "Do not worry about anything.... And the peace of God, which surpasses all understanding, will guard your hearts and minds in Christ Jesus."
(John 15 : 4) Jesus said, "Remain in me."

Prayer:
Lord, you know every fiber of our being. Please put around us people who will help us achieve the purpose for which you created us.

Session 7

Lustful Hearts

Part 1

Thomas (Tom) Wicker looked at the wall clock in his office. The time was 11:00 am. He was anxious; his heart throbbed lightly. He couldn't wait for 12:00 pm to roll in. Lunch had become a treasure worth looking forward to since he met Sasha Simms. Seated on his desk was a framed picture of his wife and three adorable children. He glanced at his family and quickly looked away. Though guilt was heavily written on his face, he mentally forced his mind back to the much anticipated lunch. He wandered back to the day it all began.

It was a rainy day; he dashed across the street from his office building to a pharmacy nearby. He went in to pick up a prescription for his 2-year old daughter. Just when he came out of the store, a car sped by, splashing muddy water on him. His grey pants were soaked below his knees and around his ankles, and he was very upset.

He was bent over, brushing down his pants when he heard a voice say, 'That's awful!' He looked up and saw what he could only classify as a beauty queen. Her smile was dazzling. He straightened up, gazing at her, momentarily lost as if something placed him under her spell.

She came towards him holding up her umbrella. "The cleaners aren't going to like that," she said, her eyes glancing over the dirt on his pants.

She was standing beside him, her umbrella partially giving him cover. His brain seemed frozen for a few seconds. "Thanks," he managed to say. His hand bobbed up and down in an attempt to show how foolish it was to come out without an umbrella. "I didn't realize the rain was this heavy when I left the office."

She looked up at the sky, and then added, "The forecast didn't predict this much rain either."

He shook his right leg, trying to dislodge the dirt on his pants. To Tom's utter amazement, she bent slightly and gently tapped his pants to get rid of the soil. He saw her delicate hand and felt guilty that she was straining such marvelously crafted fingers. He reached for her hand in an attempt to stop her. That was his downfall; it has been a long time since he held a female's soft and silky hand. He couldn't let it go. He straightened up and their eyes met. He was enticed by her essence. There was a brilliant glint in her eyes that warmed him up; he was captivated. His common sense kicked in and he realized he was holding her tight. He quickly released her and said, "You're right; the cleaners aren't going to be happy."

She shrugged. "What can one do? This is one of those things we can't control."

"Are you always this optimistic?" he asked, smiling.

"The weather already looks depressing, why add to it?" she said jovially.

Tom chuckled, nodding his head. It didn't take him long to realize that he liked her. Before he knew it, he was asking her out for lunch, to return her kindness, he managed to convince himself.

Sasha. Even the name conjured something sinful in him. During their first lunch together they had mundane conversation until their hands touched. The second time that he held her hand he was amazed at its tenderness. They were so different from Beverly's, his wife. Hers were chaffed from hours of scraping and washing. She was always doing something; either cooking, cleaning or washing. She never seemed to stop, not since they had had their three children in quick succession. Raising three children, all less than five years old, was taking a toll on their marriage.

Sasha had touched him ever so lightly. The movement had been so sensual that he felt a tingle in his loins. He couldn't stop himself from asking her out again.

This was their forth lunch together. He knew it would blow into a full affair if he didn't stop. The problem was he didn't want to stop; desire had taken root. Just the thought of meeting with her gave him so much thrill that he'd hate to give it up. The guilt came again, and he pushed it aside. In his head, he reasoned that he wasn't doing anything wrong, not yet anyway.

Losing focus on what's important can lead us to temptation. We can also be the one leading others away from the path of righteousness.

Who are you in this story?

Tom

____

____

Sasha

____

____

Part 2

Riding on a train back from work one day, Tom glanced briefly at the woman sitting next to him and then returned his gaze to the newspaper he was reading. The woman was coughing incessantly, distracting him. He shifted slightly to give her room. He was trying to avoid contact with her as he didn't want to be infected with whatever she had and then take it home. One of his children had just recovered from a cold and he didn't want to go through all the sniffling and runny noses so soon. He nearly jumped out of his skin when he felt the woman's hand on his sleeve. "May I help you?" he questioned her.

She coughed roughly before asking, "Can you help me with a couple of dollars?"

Tom saw the tracks on her arm; it was obvious that she was an illicit drug abuser. He had a low tolerance for people like her. Irritated, he answered, "Ma'am, you need to check yourself into a rehab."

"I asked you for money, not advice," she responded gruffly.

"I'm not going to support your bad habit," Tom said softly to her hearing, and then vacated the seat. Just before he exited, he heard the woman mumble, "Some think they are better than me."

He was on his way to meet Sasha for lunch the next day. His euphoric pulses were out of control, and he couldn't wait to see her. He weaved in and out of traffic, whistling to himself. He looked in the rearview mirror, and involuntarily used his tongue to sweep across his teeth. He had picked the best restaurant in town for their lunch today. All of a sudden, bam! From nowhere the voice of the woman on the train interjected in his head. Her words hit him, *"some think they are better than me."* My God! He slammed his foot on the brakes and pulled the car over. He compared himself to the woman. He was no better than her. She couldn't let go of the pleasure she derived from her drugs, which was why she didn't see the damage it was doing to herself and possibly others. Was that not the same with him? He didn't want to let go of the pleasure derived from meeting with Sasha, which would explain why he kept going back. He knew the meetings would lead to an affair which could damage his family life. Jesus! He screeched. He thought for a long time. He had advised the woman to check herself into rehab. He gave the same advice to himself. He believed the meeting was not an accident: God had sent her in his path to keep him in line. He called his church and asked for spiritual counseling.

Faith sharing:
Recall a time you've been in Tom's situation. When a desire for something unethical took root in your heart and you couldn't let go. How did you overcome it, if you did?

____

____

Reflections:

Our lustful hearts sometimes lead us astray, scheming to the point of destruction. David schemed to get Uriah killed in battle so he could marry his wife, Bathsheba. God was displeased with David, and this caused the son that Bathsheba bore for David to die (2 Samuel 11: 1-27, 12:15-17).

When we are seduced by the Evil One, he makes us believe that the things we lack are what we need. We then become obsessed to obtain these things at all costs. In the story, Tom saw in Sasha what he thought was lacking in his wife.

We should be aware that often times our struggle is not against human enemies but against principalities and the powers of evil spirits. We need the grace of God to fight back. Paul tells us to clothe ourselves with the armor of

God against the Evil One (Ephesians 6: 10-18). He lurks in every corner, waiting to devour us.

We have been commissioned to love one another. Emotions, feelings and physical attractions are only a part of that love, and if not carefully guided can lead to lust. Lust is to use another person for our selfish desires, which negates our relationship with God. In the story, Tom wanted to use Sasha's attributes to replace what his wife lacked instead of working on how to better his family life.

To love another is to firmly set our will to refuse to do anything that would reduce another person's dignity; to do only what's good for them and right in the eyes of God. When we set our eyes on Jesus, he gives us a new pair of eyes and the hold of the Evil One gets smaller.

<u>Bible Reading:</u>
(Ecclesiastes 7: 26-29) Those who please God shall escape from the snares of a woman…
(1 Peter 4:8) God's grace and love can take care of our weaknesses, failures and foibles.
(Mathew 18:3) We can let go of our anxieties and humble ourselves as God's children.
(Hebrews 11:6) God is there for all those who seek him.

Prayer:
Lord, be our refuge when addiction has a foothold on us. Give us the grace to overcome any temptation that threatens to tear our families apart. Let us not forget that we are never alone in our struggles.

Session 8

The Spirit of Discernment

Part 1

On a Sunday morning a disheveled, drunken man bought a newspaper. Head slightly bent and squinting his eyes, he scanned the headlines as he walked. As if pushed by a powerful wind, he swayed, caught himself, and hurried down the road. He came upon a church. He stood briefly at the entrance, thinking. A few times he raised his hands to knock on the door, but hesitated each time. He walked away, looking at his paper. He was plagued by a question. An idea was breaking through his head, but he couldn't focus enough to bring it forth. He turned back and banged on the church's door.

A pastor answered. He was immediately assailed by the alcoholic fumes coming from the drunkard and quickly pulled back. "How may I help you?" he asked, holding his breath.

The man didn't answer right away. With an effort he dredged up the reason for his presence. "How do you get arthritis?" he asked.

Wanting to get rid of the man quickly, the pastor didn't give much thought to the question. He answered, "You get it by drinking liquor, unhealthy diets, sexual immorality and other abuses of the body."

"Huh," the drunkard murmured. "Thank you." He cocked his head slightly and then turned to leave.

"Wait," the pastor called him back. "Why did you ask?"

The drunkard raised the front page of the newspaper

to the pastor's view and replied. "It says here that your Bishop has arthritis."

Who are you in this story?

The drunkard

____

____

The Pastor

____

____

***Part* 2**

Weeks later, with a newspaper tucked under his arm, Mr. Lee Amber came to the church. He stood aside at the entrance, observing the pastor greet several members of his congregation as they left the church building. When the last person had left, he approached the pastor and introduced himself.

The pastor warmly responded to him, returning the greetings with hearty cheers. The face looked familiar, but the pastor couldn't put a finger on where they might have met. He was sure the man was not a member of his congregation.

"You don't remember me?" Mr. Amber asked. The pastor slowly shook his head, acknowledging his uncertainty. Lifting his newspaper, Mr. Amber continued, "I came here the other day and asked about your Bishop."

Clarity came to the pastor. "Ah," he said strongly. "You look different."

Mr. Amber acknowledged that he was different from the unkempt man that once knocked on the door.

"Thanks to you," he responded.

Still a little puzzled, the pastor murmured, "How so?"

Mr. Amber pointed to his outfit, showing off his new appearance. "You changed my perception about myself the other day." As he was walking home after their last encounter he had thought the pastor was dumb. Then a thought snuck into him, telling him he was the dumb one. The pastor was not the first person to treat his appearance with disregard. He had lost some good relationships because of the way people perceived him. He had bottled up deep resentment towards them and it inadvertently manifested itself in his outward display of hostility towards life. Before meeting with the pastor, it hadn't occurred to him that he had anything to be blamed for. His reasoning had been that alcohol couldn't harm him, and hadn't fully grasped its effect on him and his social commitments. To the pastor, he said, "Your response to my question the other day was befitting my appearance. If I hadn't appeared in a drunken, disheveled state, I would have commanded more respect from you." The pastor was going to say something, but Lee raised his hand, imploring the pastor to let him finish. "I had harbored deep resentments towards people who treated me with disrespect. That day it dawned on me that I'm partly responsible. "

The pastor was dumbfounded, "Mmm," he murmured, nodding his head.

"I came to tell you I appreciate your honest answer."

The pastor began to admire his visitor; he found in him the meaning of humility. More importantly, he learned from their previous encounter that first impressions can be misleading. He had learned to probe more before opening his mouth. "You taught me a lesson too," the pastor told him. "May the savior, Jesus Christ be with you always."

Mr. Amber nodded, letting the blessing sink into his heart. He was determined to stay alcohol free. He left there feeling an inner peace that he hadn't felt in a long time.

Faith sharing:
Are there times when you've completely misjudged a situation and came up with the wrong conclusion and response?

____

____

Have you encountered someone who shed a new light into your personality? How has this encounter helped you?

____

____

Reflections:

Both men had lacked the spirit of wise discernment. The pastor didn't question the drunkard's reason for the questions before answering. Without thinking, he based his response on the man's appearance. He mistakenly responded with an inappropriate answer. The drunken man did not fit into the pastor's crowd and therefore he treated the man with disregard. Jesus tells us that we do not get credit for loving only those who love us or in this case those who are like us. He blesses us when we embrace strangers.

Mr. Amber had let his habit become who he was. He became a drunkard, instead of the righteous person that God created him to be. However, God can write with a crooked pen; through the encounter the drunken man was able to turn his life around. God promised a new life for those who turn to him (Ezekiel 36:22-28).

Mr. Amber has found a new meaning in life, which is good. However, to be successful he must be open to giving up some old things. He may even have to give up some friends, habits, and places. Jesus warns us that we cannot pour new wine into an old wineskin, the skin will burst (Mathew 9: 16-17). He instructs us to pour new wine into fresh wineskins and both will be in good condition. When we walk with the Lord, we cannot return to our old way of life, indulging in bad habits. Instead, in our new self we should strive to live righteously so that nothing can separate us from God. Don't worry. Jesus promises to give us the grace to stay in tune with him as long as we trust him.

<u>Bible Readings:</u>

(Ephesians 4: 22-24) So get rid of your old self, and must put on a new one.

(John 3: 14-18) Jesus came so that we may have wisdom from above.

(James 3: 17-18) Wisdom from above.

(Romans 8: 28) God works all things together for our good.

Prayer:

Lord, give us wisdom to know when we have faulted. Bless us with the courage to make changes, and stick with them.

Session 9

Burdened Feet

Part 1

Jim Sanders dropped his clothes at the cleaner's. He spoke briefly to the attendant on how he wanted his silk-linen blend jacket cleaned; he was afraid it might be mishandled. He then glanced at the clock. It was 7:30 am. He had just enough time to stop at Starbucks for his morning coffee and get to work at 8:00 am. He drove his latest model Lexus, weaving it through traffic. He was reciting his speech for a presentation later on at work when he saw another car cut in front of him. He slammed his hand on the horn; zong, zong! The sound was loud enough to deafen anyone close by. The car that cut in front of him almost made him rear-end into it. Not only did the driver cut through without signaling, the car also slowed, forcing Jim to slow down. He wouldn't have time to stop at Starbucks after all, he concluded. He wasn't in the best of moods, not until he has had his morning coffee.

He blasted his horn again, but it wasn't having an effect on the driver in front of him. "Damn, what a jerk!" Jim cursed. Tense and impatient, he swerved from behind the car into the road. Stepping on the brake and slowing down beside the other car, he rolled down his window and shouted, "Jerk!" From the corner of his eyes he saw an elderly man who was bent over the wheels. Who allowed these old geezers on the road? Jim wanted to know. They should be banned from driving; they should use some of that social security check on a horse-driven wagon, he thought irritably.

"Je..sus!" Jim screeched. On reflex he stepped on the brake; he almost rear-ended into a trailer truck in front of him. His heart throbbed violently and painfully. He felt a squeeze in his chest; he suddenly needed more air. He pulled on his tie, trying to loosen it; the pain progressively increased. "Jesus!" he screeched again. He remembered that he hadn't taken his medication this morning. He had rushed out of his house and thought to take it with his morning coffee when he stopped at Starbucks. Struggling to keep his eyes on the road, he reached for his briefcase. It had fallen from the seat to the floor. His hand was shaking; it looked like he wouldn't make it. He was having a heart attack. He pulled the car to the shoulder, and slumped over.

Who are you in this story?

Jim (Flustered when things didn't go his way. Temperamental, impatient, loses control and curses when habit-formed rituals are disturbed. Procrastinates; on taking his medicine)

____

____

The elderly driver (Unaware of others around him, not using rules to guide his behavior.)

____

____

Part 2

The elderly man saw that Jim had come to a complete stop and was slumped in his seat. He came out of his car and tapped lightly on the window, asking Jim to lower it.

Jim raised his head. He was breathing heavily. Still

clutching his chest, Jim inhaled deeply as air gushed in.

"Can I help you?" the old man asked.

Jim signaled to his briefcase. The man opened it and withdrew the pills where Jim indicated. Realizing that there was no liquid to swallow with the pills, the old man hurried to his car and returned with bottled water. He gave it to Jim after uncapping it. Jim drank a cupful with his medicine and rested his head on the headrest, breathing evenly.

"How do you feel?" the old man asked.

"I'll be okay in a few minutes," Jim managed to say.

"You may want to loosen anything tight-fitting."

Jim took off his tie completely.

The man went to the drive-side window. He asked Jim to open the door and sit facing him. Not sure of what the man was doing, Jim watched in utter amazement as the man removed Jim's shoes and socks, and then poured water on his feet. After a few minutes, he put Jim's socks back on him, and replaced the shoes. "Better?" he asked.

Jim didn't know if it was the pill or the bizarre things the old man did, but he felt tension eased out of him. "Thanks, I feel better," he replied.

"Good," the old man said. "Do you need an ambulance?"

"I think I can make it," Jim replied.

"Okay then," the man said. He picked up the discarded bottle and started to walk back to his car.

Still puzzled, Jim asked him, "Why did you stop, and why did you pour water on my feet?"

"I stopped because you needed help," he said jovially. His countenance changed and he got serious. "I was in a situation like yours when I was your age, and someone poured water on my feet. I didn't know why and I didn't ask." The puzzled look on Jim's face prompted him to speak further. "Years later I watched the pastor at my church wash others' feet during a Holy Thursday celebration, and then the man's action of years ago became clear. The man cleaned my feet because I had carried too much burden and lost my balance."

At the doctor's office the next day, Jim recounted how he had had a near fatal heart attack. The doctor recommended that he reduce the stresses in his life, and added that Jim was lucky the elderly man was nearby to lend a hand.

On his way home, Jim remembered his conversation with the elderly man. He wasn't a devout Christian, so the significance of Holy Thursday didn't matter to him. However, he understood how one could lose balance from being overburdened. The inference to the feet was that they carried the rest of the body, and could be weakened by excessive weight. An analogous deduction could be that one who carried too much on their mind (or was self-absorbed) became weak in making swift and sound decisions. Washing could be an analogy for removing unnecessary loads, distractions, or stressors. Another insight that came to him was that despite his haughty behavior towards the elderly man, the man had stopped to lend a helping hand. That was awesome, and what a lesson! Jim thought. He saw the goodness in the elderly man, and surmised that God must be like that. Jim felt humbled, thinking he had some serious adjustments to make in his life. He would sure tell his friends about this.

What were Jim's excess loads?

____

____

The elderly man's?

How could they reduce their burdens?

Faith Sharing:

Do you remember a time you lost control because you had too much on your mind?

What excess load do you carry?

How can you remove/reduce them?

<u>Reflections:</u>

We are called to humility which comes from accepting things as they are and looking to God for clarity. The fundamental truth is that God is loving and merciful; he has filled us with his likeness, and commissioned us to show it to one another.

Jesus washed the disciple's feet (John 13: 5-17). A symbolic event: Jesus loved them enough to lower himself to wash the lowest part of their body. This is an example of his life's message; a sign of humility. He tells us that we should not be too self-righteous that we cannot lower ourselves to help another in need.

God has appointed duties to everyone and wants us to have mutual recognition for the good in each of us as we journey through life. In his abundance, he blessed us with different gifts and talents. We are to use these gifts to better ourselves and others.

God is love; he made us for loving. Our resolutions should be that no stress, worries or pain can separate us from that love. Jesus went as far as to tell us that if our hand causes us to sin, we should cut it off, it is better to have one hand than be thrown into hell with two hands. This is how serious Jesus takes our relationship with God. Our body parts are vital to the functions of our bodies, yet we are told to get rid of them if they obstruct our reaching intimacy with God. He loves us and wants us to return that love with a childlike innocence, free of worries.

Bible Reading:
(Isaiah 7 :10-14) Even when we're unwilling, God can bring His awesome presence to us. He is patient. Ahaz refused to ask God for a sign, and He gave Ahaz the sign anyway.
(John 13: 3-5) Jesus is here to cleanse us. He washed the disciples' feet. He did this to wash away their fears and doubts. He sent them filled with the spirit and light on their feet to evangelize and alleviate others of their fears. The less our burden , the quicker our feet will move to proclaim the good news of God's kingdom.
(Micah 6:6-8) What the lord requires of us.
(James 2:14-26) Faith and actions.

Prayer:

Lord, so many times we have taken our eyes away from you. We occupy our minds with things we have no control over. Help us to slow down, admire the expanse that is your creation, listen to the birds that sing, hear the ripples in the winds that grace our ears, and be joyous for our heartbeat that reminds us that you have placed us on earth one more day because you love us so much.

Session 10

The Afflicted Hearts

(Adapted from Hatcher's Room -Men Only by Caroline Ilogienboh)

Part 1

Theo Johnson walked into the lobby of his apartment building. The security guard stopped him, signaling to a female who sat on a lone chair in the foyer.

"Who is that?" Theo asked the guard.

"She didn't say. She said she has an appointment with you. I told her to wait there."

Theo walked towards the female. She looked up, saw Theo and shot to her feet.

"Hi, Detective." She smiled. "My name is Abby. Do you remember me?"

"Abby," Theo repeated slowly. He didn't recollect her. "No, I don't."

"You arrested my boyfriend about two months ago after he ran away with our son. I came to tell you how grateful I am."

"In my apartment building?"

"It's private, and I didn't think you'd mind." She flashed him a smile.

Puzzled, Theo asked. "How did you find me?'"

"I followed you."

His instincts told him this was going to be one of those scenes that cops hate; a liberated prey who ends up stalking the rescuer. If it weren't a job requirement that he live within the county zone, he'd have moved, putting a good distance between him and people like this. "This isn't necessary," he said coolly. "I was doing my job."

Abby laughed bashfully, and then slowly slithered close to Theo. She ran her finger down his sleeve. "I also want to know you better," she said smoothly.

The suggestive moves were overt. "You better go, Miss." He nudged her towards the door.

"I really want you to be my baby's daddy," she added quickly, giving Theo a seductive smile.

Astonished, Theo glared at her. "You what?" If looks could kill, he'd have been down for first-degree murder. "You can leave the same way you came." He pointed to the front door, and walked towards the elevator.

Abby ran after him, jumping inside the elevator before the door closed. He shoved his thumb on the open-button, asking her to leave. Instead of leaving, she was more determined to pursue her purpose; she threw herself on him. He edged away from her, pushing her at arms length. They tussled and he finally pushed her out of the elevator. The door closed.

"Be my baby's daddy. I love you," Abby yelled.

Theo faintly heard her. "In your dreams," he mumbled. His cell phone rang as soon as he stepped into his apartment. This had better be important, he thought as he yanked the phone from his jacket. "Hello."

"Hi, Son."

"Hi, Mom."

"I'm heading to Center City, and I have someone I want you to meet," Mrs. Johnson said wittily.

He knew what this was about. His mother has been trying effortlessly to find him a bride. "Mom, you have to stop hooking me up with every single female in Philly."

"I want some grand-babies. I'll bring her to your place. We should be there in half an hour."

"No, Mom. I'm still at work, and I'll be here for hours," he lied.

Mrs. Johnson laughed, ignoring Theo's protest. "I'll see you soon." She hung up.

Sorry, mom, not today. He'd rather be in the company of his friends. He quickly changed his work clothes to something casual and rushed out of the apartment.

We sometimes go to the extreme to get what we want, or impress our desires on others or run from confronting uncomfortable situations.

Who are you in this story?

Theo

____

____

Abby

____

____

Mrs. Johnson

____

____

***Part* 2**

Theo entered Arthur's Café and walked straight to the bar. The bartender passed him a water bottle and told him that the men were at the back. Theo uncapped the bottle as he headed to the back room. Five men were already seated around a table with cards spread among them. Mike Vatiano dangled an unlit cigar between his lips. John Connor held up his cards, and took a swig from a glass simultaneously. Jesse Brunel tipped a Martini in his mouth, welcoming Theo with a nod of his head. Akin Badesola tapped on the table, nudging Jesse to lay down his cards. Sean Martin wiped his mouth with the back of his hand, and motioned Theo to sit in an empty chair beside him. Theo dropped jadedly into the chair.

John gave Theo a curious look. "You okay?" he asked.

Theo narrated his encounters. "I'm pissed right now," he growled.

"Why is it that women think they can control our lives?" John asked brashly.

"How about the ones who want to have your baby and later want to kill you because you don't care about them?" Sean threw in. "My two babies' mothers are after me now. I didn't promise them anything. I don't understand why they want to tear me to pieces."

"Or the ones who spend every dime you make and still call you worthless," Mike added gloomily. " I bought my wife a BMW. She got in the car and drove off without telling me where she was going. She came back four hours later. When I asked her where she went, you know what she said?" Everyone looked at him expectantly, waiting for him to supply the answer. "She said 'just because you bought me a car is no reason to question my movement.'" Mike shook his head. "What kind of an answer is that? Don't you agree that I have the right to know?" His head bobbed right and left, seeking support.

"How about my wife who slept with another man while I was at work, sweating to make money for the family?" Jesse butted in. His voice was tight, an indication of how upset he was. "You break your neck for them and they repay you with grief."

"My wife got me arrested in front of my own children. How heartless is that? "Akin asked. "I'll never forgive her."

Sean looked around before adding,"Hector is not here yet, but I speak for him. His ex-wife should go to hell. While they were still married, he came home one day and she told him she was in love with someone else. Come to find out, she was in love with another woman."

"You know if Hector was here, he'd be in tears right now," Jesse said, glancing at the empty chair next to him.

"Do you blame him? She stripped the man of his dignity. He should cry if he wants to. Men have feelings too," John asserted.

"As long as he doesn't do it in front of a woman, he can cry all he wants," Mike threw in.

"The last thing any of us need is to be called weak," Akin mouthed.

"I just wish they'd leave me alone, including my mother," Theo interjected resonantly.

"Women want us to take care of them, and when you say something they don't want to hear, they call you a male chauvinistic pig. I'm not a pig when money flows from my pocket," John rejoined. "That's why we come here where they can't bother us."

"Yeah," a couple of voices resounded.

The backroom of Arthur's Café became a place for men after the owner went through a messy divorce. He had been in dire emotional pain. One day he found another man who had had similar experiences. Together they shared their stories, had some drinks and some good belly laughs. Soon other men began to join. The gathering born out of misery, disappointments, resentments, anger, or whatever ugly mix life has dumped on the men's paths became some sort of support group. They discussed anything from the opposite sex to sports and politics. Membership was open to all regardless of race, religion, or economic status. They had one thing in common: bitterness towards women.

What do these men need?

Suggest an action plan, followed by a scripture verse for each man?

Theo:____

Mike:____

John:____

Sean:____

Jesse:____

Hector:____

Akin:____

Hector joined the group later that evening. His demeanor was unlike what the men have seen; he had a smile on his face. This was unusual; the men stared at him with a puzzling look on their faces.

"Did you win a lottery?" John directed the question at Hector.

"No," Hector answered with cheer resounding at the

base of his voice. The stares nudge him to share the cause of his good mood. To answer his friends, he said, "I saw my ex-wife."

"Oh her!" Sean dismissed Hector's admission with a wave of his hand.

"Go on," John interjected.

"I really looked at her, and she looked better than I have seen in years," Hector continued. "She then told me how unhappy she was when we were married. That was why we had so many arguments before she left." Hector chuckled before adding, "Guys, for all the tears I have shed after the breakup, it never occurred to me that she too was miserable. My recent encounter with her was an eye-opener. In my heart I couldn't hate this woman; instead I told her I was glad for her new found happiness." His eyes scanned the room to see if they were following him. "You know what the best part is?" Everyone waited for him to provide the answer. He didn't want to reveal that he got tired of living in misery; that he had resorted to praying and found comfort in speaking with God. He simply said, "I walked away with a sense of relief. I've been in a great mood since then."

"Does this mean we won't be seeing you anymore," Sean asked.

"It feels good not to carry all that bitterness around," Hector replied. "You are my friends, and I want you to experience it too. I'm going to stick around until everyone comes to this awesome feeling."

Faith sharing:
"Misery loves company"
Can you recall a time when you had a problem and sought out friends who had similar problems. Did the experience help you?

Have you stayed around friends to share God's amazing grace when a problem suddenly lifts off of you?

What do you think happened to Hector at the encounter with his ex-wife?

Can you think of possible explanations for Hector's reluctance to speak about his relationship with God?

"I'm going to stick around until everyone comes to this awesome feeling." To keep this promise, suggest ways that Hector might introduce God to this group.

Reflections:

Life can seem unfair sometimes. Jesus cares about the things that trouble us. He invites the weary to come, and he will give them rest (Matthew 11: 28-30). He proved that he is accessible when a man with a dreaded skin disease asked Jesus to make him clean if he wants to (Mathew 8:1-4). Without hesitation Jesus replied,"I want to." The man was an outcast and alone; Jesus reached out to him and cured him. Jesus' outpour of compassion and response was instantaneous. His desire to come to our aid is like that, on autopilot. He is extremely pleased when we turn to him for help.

We do not want to be like the people of Gadara (Matthew 8:28-33), who begged Jesus to leave their territory after he healed two men possessed by a legion of demons. The people missed out on a great opportunity to see miracles beyond their imagination when they didn't believe in Jesus. Instead, we are to come to him like the woman who hemorrhaged for twelve years (Luke 8:43-48). Fearlessly, she approached Jesus and was healed.

The heavenly father has put all things under his power (John 13:3), and he is ready to vanquish all that threatens our existence. In our hopelessness we may not even know exactly what kind of healing we need, but he does. In the story above, Hector found freedom when his way of thinking changed. The powers of the Holy Spirit gave him new eyes to see.

We are companions in life's journey and are called to recognize the goodness in each other; encouraging in bad times, lending a hand in difficult situations, joyous in good times, correcting in times of deviation from righteousness, and helping each other be the people we are supposed to be. Share God's steadfast love; sharing helps us to grow in union with the father.

When we pray and spend time with the Lord we receive love, wisdom, knowledge and everything deemed right by the father. Jesus promises us that when two or more are gathered in his name he will be there. He invites us to come to his well and drink to our hearts' content. Rejoice, brothers, harden not your hearts. God who created us in his image has mapped out every life in the palm of his hands. Our daily resolutions should thus be:

ACTS

A- Acknowledging God for his omnipotent presence.

C- Contrition, being sorry for the sins that put a wedge between us and him.

T- Thanking him for all his blessings.
S- Supplication; praying for all our needs according to his will.

Bible Reading:
(Psalm 105) God keeps his promise to his people.
(John 17 :1-11) Jesus glorifies the father. He shows the flow of love from the father to the son; back and forth. We are also included in that outpour.
(Romans 8: 6) To be controlled by the Spirit leads to life and peace.
(Philippians 3 :12-14) Run towards the goal.

Prayer:

In you Lord, we lay our troubled souls. Deliver us from hardness of hearts and protect us from anxieties. Division among us pulls us away from you. Keep our relationships safe from the gnawing hands of the Evil One.

Session 11

That I Might Bring Mirth to Others.
(Adapted from Jayda's Story- Lost at the Crossroads by Caroline Ilogienboh)

Part 1

For an agonized 14-year-old, Jayda Wills running away from home seemed the only option. Lost and confused, she found refuge in a dingy apartment that was like a match-box for the eight inhabitants. Among them was Selina Hutton, who one day shared her story with Jayda.

"My mother died when I was eleven," Selina began. "I never knew who my father was. I was placed in several foster homes, until they found the right one for me. Everything was fine for the first two years. My foster mother was real cool. Her brother lost his job and came to live with us, and soon he started to visit me at night. When I protested, he told me no one would believe me. He was right."

"You didn't tell anyone?" asked Jayda.

"Yeah," answered Selina. "I told my foster mother. She laughed and said I had imagined everything. She didn't believe that her sweet brother was capable of what I was accusing him. She warned me not to repeat it to anyone. I kept quiet because I was afraid that I'd be moved to another foster home. It went on for another year until I found out that I was pregnant and ran away."

"Where did you go?"

"I hid in a church basement for a month."

"No one saw you?"

"The pastor's wife caught me one day. She rained

curses on me and threw cans of tuna at me. I ran out as fast as I could before she called the police."

"Didn't she see that you were pregnant?"

"Sometimes, people can't see beyond their anger."

"What happened next?"

"I stayed here and there until one day I went into a grocery store and stole bananas and some other stuff. The store manager called the police. Before I knew what hit me, I was hauled off in a police car. They found out that I was pregnant and called social services. I was placed in a shelter until the baby was born and adopted. I only saw her once. I'll never forget how small she looked. She was so fragile, like a baby doll. I was scared to touch her; I told the nurse to take her away before I gave her my bad luck. The social worker later told me that they'd find a nice home for her and not to worry. I had no choice but to believe her." She paused. "When I left the hospital, I went back to the shelter. Two months later they told me that they found another foster home for me. I begged them to let me stay where I was, but they refused. They said I was fourteen and needed a family. I laughed at them and went out the back door. They never saw me again."

"Where did you go?"

"I spent a lot of time walking around town. At night I hid in the basement of a restaurant."

"How did you become a singer?"

"One night I was going through the bar's trash when a girl saw me. She asked me what I was looking for. I started to run and she ran after me. I ran out of breath and she caught up with me. She asked me why I was running when she only asked what I was looking for. She seemed nice, so I told her that I was hungry. She begged me to come back with her; that she'd get me food from the kitchen. Reluctantly, I followed her. She brought me some food and we started to talk. She was sixteen years old and living with her boyfriend. Her boyfriend worked with the band, and she thought I could be a good singer if I worked at it. Her name is Yvonne. She asked me to move in with them; she taught me a lot. I've been singing since."

"Boy! I thought I had problems," Jayda blurted out with her mouth agape. "How did you survive?"

"I guess God was looking out for me," Selina responded, smiling. She nudged Jayda's shoulder and said, "He is looking out for you too?"

The troubled teen looked doubtful. "I don't know, Ms. Selina," she said with reservation.

"Believe me, I once had doubts and He proved that nothing is impossible for him to do. I'm a living witness."

Who are you in this story?

Selina (Witnessing and sharing God's amazing work in her life.)

____

____

The pastor's wife (Lacking in the spirit of compassion when she couldn't see pass her anger.)

____

____

Yvonne (Not giving up; chasing after the broken and hungry to offer comfort and hope.)

____

____

Jayda (Deep in pain, in search of self-discovery. Doubtful of God's mercies.)

____

Part 2

Jayda lay on the couch, closed her eyes and drifted into sleep.

"Nana, Nana, look!" Jayda said to her grandmother. "Your hat is not falling off my head!" She looked in the mirror while adjusting a blue hat on her head.

"You better hurry up child," Nana responded firmly. "Church starts in half an hour."

"Look at the hat, Nana. It fits!" Jayda announced merrily.

"Didn't I tell you to stay out of my things?"

"It's so beautiful and the color goes with my dress," Jayda muttered, turning sideways to face her grandmother.

Nana stood at the door shaking her head. She thought of how headstrong the child could be when she wanted something.

"See, see," Jayda said, whirling around.

"It looks good on you," Nana said, smiling.

"Can I? Please Nana, I'll take care of it, promise."

"You'll keep it on your head?"

"Yes!"

"Now hurry up, let's go."

Nana picked up her handbag and walked out of the house. Jayda ran behind her, holding the hat firmly against her ears.

"Nana, wait," Jayda screeched. "You're walking too fast."

"You know I have to be at choir practice before the service starts. Move those skinny legs of yours. I have no time to wait." Nana walked briskly, pulling Jayda's hand along. At the entrance of the church they heard the organ playing some melody. The choir was already assembled and singing. Nana joined and took her position. Jayda sat in the front pew and sang along,

"Lift me high
When I'm down, lift me higher
When I fall, lift me higher, higher
Lord, lift me high, higher and higher."

The morning sun warmed her face and she slowly opened her eyes with a lazy grin. From deep within she hummed, and then stretched her limbs. Her lips moved involuntarily. *"Lift me high. Lift me higher, and higher."*

"Are you singing?" Selina asked with a surprised gaze.

"Oh! I just woke up," Jayda said, smiling.

"You're in a good mood!"

"I guess so. Is it okay if I go to church today?"

"Sure!" Selina was glad the girl was taking the step. "Maybe you can stop at home too," she added lightly. "Your family must be worried sick about you."

After some thoughtful moments, Jadya responded, "I think I will."

Faith sharing:
Have you ever been in a situation where someone else shared their life's story and it gave you hope?

____

____

<u>Reflections:</u>

Our predicaments would sometimes make us believe there is hopelessness in the situation we find ourselves.

Our minds become distraught, fearful and lost. We may even denounce the existence of God, feeling safer buried in our troubles. Jesus says not to worry. Look at the birds; they do not plant seeds or harvest and store up in a barn, yet the heavenly father takes care of them. You are worth more than the birds. He will surely take care of you. (Mathew 6:25-34).

How do we lose our doubting nature and become believers?
By:

- Reflecting on God's favors in our lives through our experiences.
- When sudden burdens have been lifted from our shoulders
- When our prayers have been answered.
- Listening to another's account of God's mercies.

Bible Readings:
(Isaiah 43: 1-5) God's promise to be with his people.
(John 20:24-31) Thomas doubted Jesus' resurrection. Jesus invited him to come closer and stop doubting.
(Mathew 8: 5-17) The Centurion had no doubts about Jesus' power and authority; he got his heart's desire.
(Romans 10:9) We will be saved if we confess that Jesus is the Lord.
(Luke 1:29-31) The fulfillment of God's promise: Mary was deeply troubled by the angel's message and she wondered what his words meant. The angel said to her, "Don't' be afraid, Mary..."

Prayer:

Lord, let us be your messengers to others. May we show your glory by what we do and say. By our actions let us lead others to you.

Session 12

When All Else Fails

Part 1

David Stelle approached the church with fierce anxiety. His fingers curled into his palms and his feet became heavily laden. A voice whispered in his head, 'Don't go in, they do not welcome people like you.' For a brief moment his wastrel life flashed in front of him, and he didn't like what he saw. With an effort, he tuned out the voice, telling himself he'd take the chance. He stood rooted at the entrance; the willpower that had led him thus far suddenly vanished. The internal debate began again; he was a loser, he had gambled his life away. His wife has locked him out of their bedroom, his children looked at him with distrust, and his foreclosure notice poked out of his pocket. On this Sunday morning, he had set out to his parent's home and remembered that they probably would not be there. His feet followed the path he knew they'd have gone like they had done in the past forty years. His parents were devout Christians; neither rain nor shine could stop them from going to church on a Sunday.

David had rebelled against that very upbringing the minute he left home. To his parent's disappointments, he hadn't stepped in a church in twenty years. The urgency in his present situation had forced him to this very door. A still voice told him to turn around and go home. He turned to leave, and then heard, "The Lord hears the cry of the poor, blessed be the Lord." He swerved around, frowning. He was sure he had heard his mother's voice.

His feet moved involuntarily into the church and he sat unnoticed at the back pew. He wondered what he was doing there; he did not belong with all these nice people dressed in their Sunday best. He shifted in an attempt to leave again, but something held him down.

His thoughts drifted to when he was young and his father had lost his job of nineteen years due to the downsizing at his company. His father had taken the lay-off badly. He began to stay back in church after the service to pray. The family would wait anxiously in the car. David hated the wait; it used to annoy him because he wanted to get home to eat his Sunday morning pancakes, bacon, and sausages and read the comics in the newspaper. He had been fourteen then, and in his impatience had asked his father why he wasted so much time praying. His father had responded with 'Son, when all else fails, you turn to God.' Thinking about that phrase now made him relax and he sat through the service. At the end, he was about to quietly slip out when he felt someone pull his shoulder. His uncle, Brad Stelle, pulled and hugged him.

"Where have you been?" he asked sharply. "We haven't seen you in years."

"Hi, Uncle Brad," David responded.

"Your mother has been worried about you," the uncle held David's hand captive while he visually searched the congregation for MaryAnn, David's mother. "MaryAnn!" he called when he saw her.

"Dave, how are you?" Juliet Stelle, Brad's wife asked as she joined her husband.

"You can see he is as messy as we've all heard," the uncle provided an answer. "The boy disappointed all of us."

His wife pulled him aside, "This is not the time," she whispered. "Lay off him."

MaryAnn pushed through the crowd towards them. She was surprised to see David in church. "My God!" she yelped. "I thought I'd never see this day." She came forward, laying her frail hands on her son.

"Hi, mom," David greeted her. He was a little awkward and clumsily accepted his mother's display of affection that was mixed with tears. He hugged her tight.

She disengaged and visually searched the crowd. "Where's your father?" She waved to him on sighting him.

"David!" George, David's father hollered. Unlike his mother whose face wetted with tears on the reunion, the father stood sternly, watching his son closely with a puzzled frown.

"Say something," MaryAnn nudged her husband.

"How are you, son?" he asked.

Nodding slowly, David answered, "Can we go home?"

"I agree," the uncle interjected. "No point broadcasting that the prodigal son has returned. There aren't going to be any fatted cows killed for him. You all should go home." He grabbed David's hand, shaking it lightly. "Clean up nephew, and stay close to home." He departed with his wife.

"Let's go home." MaryAnn said to David and his father.

Who are you in this story?

David (Had internal debate; afraid to approach the Lord in time of trouble.)

____

____

Uncle Brad (Judgmental, brash and unruly with his tongue.)

Juliet (Stepped in to prevent criticism and inflicting more pain on another.)

MaryAnn (Openly displays her unconditional love.)

George (Couldn't come up with the appropriate words to address the situation.)

Part 2

At his parent's house, David reflected on how he came to seek them out. He had taken his four-year-old son, Max to see his pre-school teacher a few days earlier. As they waited in the small conference room he had noticed coffee stain on his tie. It made his attire look sloppy, and this was not the impression he wanted to give Ms. Anders, Max's teacher. Dissatisfied with his appearance, he had muttered 'Jesus Christ!' to his son's hearing. Max held up his index finger against his lips and whispered, 'Shh, shh, don't' say that, dad.' He gave Max a questioning look. The boy lowered his voice and added, 'Anytime you say 'Jesus Christ!' you usually have an argument with mom afterwards. I don't want you arguing with my teacher. I'm already in trouble for not doing my homework.' His son's statement remained with him long after the conference was over.

In that small room, it dawned on him that Max had

learned to identify the name of Jesus with a negative behavior so much that the boy cowered at the proclamation. This was not what he wanted to teach his son; the implication pointed him out as a bad father. It further compounded the mess he found himself in, and it was the last straw. He was deeply troubled and didn't know what to do. He finally sought out his parents.

Coming out of a reverie, David confided to his father that his gambling began when he started playing the lotto. It was a weekly pastime and he enjoyed scratching the ticket for a winning number. He played with a small amount, so it didn't put a dent in his pocket. His winning streaks went down and he became anxious. One day, a friend introduced him to betting on horses. They went to a race track and he started betting with big money. He even went as far as taking money from their bank account without his wife's knowledge. He promised to put the money back, but unfortunately he could never win enough to replace what he had taken. He started spending more and more time at the track. His finances went on a downward spiral. He was now in deep debt, which had led to heated arguments with his wife. His family was hurting. He didn't understand how he had deviated so much from the good nurturing his parents had given him; he hated himself.

George saw anguish in his son's eyes and it pained him. He knew what David needed. A phrase popped in his head, "We are restless until we rest in God." His son needed God's mercy. He wondered if David was ready to do what it takes. He recalled the event in the bible when a rich young man approached Jesus. To David, he said, "A rich young man went to Jesus on his knees wanting to know how to receive eternal life. Jesus told him to sell his things and give the proceeds to the poor."

"I remember it," David interjected. "The young man went away very sad because he didn't want to part with his riches."

"Yes!" George's face lit up, he was happy that David hadn't forgotten all his Sunday school teachings. "I'm telling you this because the young man was more attached to his riches than to God. You, my son became attached to gambling. As you have found out, attachment to earthly things does not grant happiness." Lowering his voice, he added, "Don't go away sad like the young man. Come back to church and rest in God. He will give you the graces to forgive yourself and set you on the right path."

"Thanks, dad," David said. "I'm glad I came to you."

George gazed at his son; he was filled with joy. He thought this must be how the father of the lost son felt when his son returned home. He prayed for the Holy Spirit to direct his son's life.

David left his parents' house full of hope.

Faith sharing:

Have you ever been in a situation when you want to do right and a voice in your head tries to convince you to do otherwise?

____

____

<u>Reflections</u>

In times of trouble, we sometimes distance ourselves from others even when we need help. We're convinced that we don't want others to know our problems either because we fear they'd judge us harshly or we are ashamed. We wallow in our pains, giving the Evil One more power to fester in our hearts. We can break the chains of slavery and reach out for help. Talk to trusted family members or friends. Even in the process of venting our inner fears and frustrations we can let go of self-recriminations that hold us down, and let new ideas flow in.

God in his mercy will send the Holy Spirit to breathe new life into us. Jesus is anxiously waiting for us to bring our troubles to him. Don't let the dryness in your life hold you down. Elijah prayed for rain. He put faith in God, and water poured down from heaven (1 King 18:45). Things may look bleak now, hope and trust in God. He will surely pour down his blessings. It may not come when we want it or in the form we expect, but it will come in God's own perfect time.

Bible Readings

(Mark 10: 17-27) The rich young man.
(Luke 15: 11-24) The lost son.
(James 3: 1-12) Beware with the tongue.
(Galatians 5: 13-26, 6: 1-10) Do not be led by the desires of the flesh and do good to others.
(Mathew 11: 28-30) Jesus invites all those who are weary, and promises to give them rest, for the yoke he gives is light.

Prayer:

When in distress, Lord, let us turn to you. You are the rock of our foundation. Whether in pain, lost or alone, your sweet compassion is all we desire. Let us not forget that you are our refuge and your well never dries. All we have to do is come to you and drink to our hearts content. Thank you for loving us first.

Stay Connected

The church community is like a bicycle wheel: a circular metal frame with several spokes coming from the circumference to connect at the centre. If one spoke disconnects from the center, the wheel looses its balance. If all are connected, there's harmony and a smooth ride. In this analogy, Jesus is the center of the church, we are the spokes. Our lives retain a balance when we stay connected to him. Jesus asks us to remain in him so that our joy may be complete (John 15:9-17).

Like the widow of Zarephath whose bowl did not run out of flour and her jar of oil did not run out, we will never run out of God's goodness (1 Kings 17: 8-16).

We pray for the gifts of wisdom, understanding, counsel, knowledge, fortitude, piety, and the fear of God (Isaiah: 11:2).

We pray to the Holy Spirit to renew us with eyes that see and ears that hear so that we can bear fruits of love, joy, serenity, endurance, gentleness, goodness, and faith (Galatians 5: 22-26).

"Who, then, can separate us from the love of Christ (Romans 8:35)?" …"For I am certain that nothing can separate us from his love: neither death nor life, neither angels nor other heavenly rulers or powers, neither present nor the future, neither the world above nor the world below- there is nothing in all creation that will ever be able to separate us from the love of God which is ours through Christ Jesus our Lord (Romans 8 38-39)."

By our daily tasks we pray to use our lives to advance God's kingdom. In Jesus Christ we'll grow and him in us. We'll go where his love leads us until eternity when we meet him face to face.

References:

- Crossing the Threshold of Hope by His Holiness John Paul II, Edited by Virttorio Messori

- Good News Bible, Today's English Version, American Bible Society

- Great Christian Thinkers, by Hans Küng

- Concerning the City of God against the Pagans, Saint Augustine, Translated by Henry Bettenson

- The Confessions of Saint Augustine, Translated by Edward B. Pusey

- Healing Wounded Emotions_ Overcoming Life's Hurts, Martin H. Padovani

Other books by the author:

- Young Adult Trilogy:
  - **Jayda's Story- Lost at the Crossroads**
    ISBN 0-9712781-0-5 @ $9.99
    Running away from home seems like the only solution to Jayda Wills' problems. Little did she know that life on the run has its own troubles.
    -Jayda's Story- Discussion Workbook
  - **The Return of Tyreek** ISBN 0-9712781-3-X @ $14.99
    To Tyreek Jackson, drug trafficking is a business. Undeterred by incarceration, he would supply as long as there is a demand. Then one day he is on the run from an assailant. He finds refuge in the home of a former drug addict, Alyssa Spence whose struggles with her biracial identity had led her from her suburban community to the hood. The dealer and the addict, the tables are turned. Tyreek's survival would depend on the unusual alliance, and Jayda's love.
    - The Return of Tyreek -Discussion Workbook
  - **Nowhere to Hide** ISBN 0-9712781-4-8 @$14.95
    In search of her identity, Izzy Martinez takes on today's popular culture. Her parents' solution for the cultural shock is a one way ticket to Puerto Rico, but they'd have to find her first. In her flight she ends up in the hands of a street gang. Everything goes eerie when Izzy rescues a gang member, Jamal Bricks from execution. The two must now join forces to stay alive. Their only hope of survival is Jayda and Tyreek.

- **I heard Your Call- A Collection of Poems & Stories in Remembrance of 9/11/ 2001** ISBN 0-9712781-2-1 @$4.99
- **Hatcher's Room- Men Only** ISBN 978-0-9712781-6-5 @ $19.99
  Arthur's café is a place of solace for the seven men that gathered there weekly. Their bitterness towards women is palpable in their weekly discussions. Separate, each man fights his own demons. Could they reach deep into their hearts to find what really plagues them? It's a question they grapple with. The key to their serenity lay in the hands of the very women they detest.

- **Saving Bekyah- Confronting Female Circumcision, Sexuality & Womanhood** By Caroline Omoifo
  ISBN 978-0-9712781-7-2 Hardcover @ $22.95

  A torturous cry rose from the depth of her being, piercing the sky. Even the gods could no longer turn a deaf ear to it. They looked down and asked, "O daughter of the earth, who shall we send?"

  In a remote village in Africa, Bekyah Tage shivered with fear. Looming over her was a razor that would sear her private part in an aged practice of (*Ureh*) female circumcision. Could she be saved? The villagers would fight any intruder in order to preserve their tradition.

  Enter Candice Zakeih, a US-based daughter of the land. Having suffered the indignity and aftereffects of the procedure herself, she'd put her American life on hold to save the little girl from the *Ureh*. She confronted the local establishment, her family and kin. The people who once welcomed her with open arms became fierce enemies. They devised dangerous ploys to remove her from their mix. Undeterred, she unfolds the reality of *Ureh* on sexuality, physiology, psychology and spirituality.

  Like a lone soldier she fought back, drawing strength from a prior encounter with her boss, Kesson Davone, in Madrid, Spain. To back her cause was a surprise visit by several associates from the United States, and other concerned citizens, mostly men, who could no longer remain indifferent to the effects of the *Ureh*. Resolution was finally achieved through a collaborative negotiation.

Notes:

Notes:

Notes:

Notes: